The King's New Clothes

Written and Illustrated by
Robin Koontz

King Crock loved clothes. He always had new clothes for every day of the week. But King Crock was not sure who he could trust.

One day two tailors came to visit the king.
"We can create a magic robe that will save
your kingdom!" they said.

"What kind of robe can save my kingdom?" asked King Crock.

"The people you can trust will see a beautiful robe," said one tailor.

"What will the other people see?" asked King Crock.

"They will see a big black and white skunk," said the other tailor.

7

King Crock liked the idea. If someone held their nose or ran when they saw his magic robe, he would know they could not be trusted.

The king hired the tailors. Then he invited the entire kingdom to attend a special party.

A few days before the party, King Crock went to see his magic robe.

"See how beautiful it is," said one tailor as he held up the robe.

"It shimmers with rainbow colors!" said the other tailor proudly.

King Crock saw a furry black cape with white stripes.

"Oh dear," he thought. "It looks like a big skunk!
Can I not trust my own eyes?"

"It is the most beautiful robe I have ever seen," King Crock said as the tailors wrapped the robe over his shoulders.

"Magnificent!" cried the tailors. The king's attendants agreed. They did not want their king to think that they could not be trusted.

On the day of the party, King Crock entered the grand jungle wearing his magic robe.

The party guests all stared. Then one held her nose. Then another, then another.

Soon everyone ran away, including the king's attendants.

"Is there no one in my kingdom I can trust?"
cried King Crock. He sat on his throne and sighed.

"I won't run away." said a wee voice.

"Oh, hello," said King Crock. From then on, the skunk and King Crock became trusting friends and lived happily ever after.

After Reading Activities

You and the Story...

Why did the king want the magic robe?

Which animal became the king's trusting friend?

How do you know which friends you can trust?

Tell a friend why you trust him or her.

Words You Know Now...

Write a sentence on a piece of paper using 3 of the words you know now. Can you write another sentence using 3 different words from the list below?

attendants	magnificent	tailors
ballroom	proudly	trust
create	shoulders	
kingdom	special	

You Could...Plan Your Own Special Party

- Make a list of the friends you will invite to your party. Will you only invite people you can trust?

- Create invitations for your party. Make sure the invitations tell:
  - What the party is for
  - What your guests need to bring
  - The date and time of your party
  - The location of the party

- What will you do at your party?

About the Author and Illustrator

Robin Koontz loves to write and illustrate stories that make kids laugh. Robin lives with her husband and various critters in the Coast Range mountains of western Oregon. She shares her office space with Jeep the dog, who gives her most of her ideas.

www.rourkeeducationalmedia.com

Edited by Luana K. Mitten
Illustrated by Robin Koontz
Art Direction and Page Layout by Renee Brady

Library of Congress Cataloging-in-Publication Data

Koontz, Robin
 The King's New Clothes / Robin Koontz.
     p. cm. -- (Little Birdie Books)
 ISBN 978-1-61741-824-2 (hard cover) (alk. paper)
 ISBN 978-1-61236-028-7 (soft cover)
 Library of Congress Control Number: 2011924705

Printed in China, FOFO I - Production Company
   Shenzhen, Guangdong Province

Ruurke
Educational Media

rourkeeducationalmedia.com

customerservice@rourkeeducationalmedia.com • PO Box 643328 Vero Beach, Florida 32964

Words to Know Before You Read

attendants

ballroom

create

kingdom

magnificent

proudly

shoulders

special

tailors

trust